The Chaotic Mind

FanatiXx Publication

ISO 9001:2015 CERTIFIED

The Chaotic Mind

FanatiXx Publication
AM/56, Basanti Colony, Rourkela 769012, Odisha
ISO 9001:2015 CERTIFIED
Website: *www.fanatixx.in*

"The Chaotic Mind"

By: Annie. J. Kathy

ISBN: 978-93-89557-45-9

Collection of English Poems & Quotes 1st Edition

Book Formatting: Saizal Gupta

Cover Design: Sornojoy Dutta

Disclaimer

2

This is a work of fiction. The characters, places, organization's and events described in this book are either a work of author's imagination, or purely her life experiences or have been used fictitiously. Any resemblance to people, living or dead, places, events, communities or organization's is purely coincidental.

The quotes and poems in this book are solely written by its writer. If any plagiarism is found later, the Publication will not be responsible.

Acknowledgement

"THANK YOU" is the best prayer that anyone could say. I say that one a lot. Thank you expresses extreme gratitude, humility, understanding

– Alice Walker

First and the foremost I would like to thank my God Almighty for bestowing his blessings upon me and making my dreams come true. I am eternally grateful to my parents who have been my backbone and supporting me till date and encouraging me in all my endeavors. I would like to thank my teachers who kindled the hidden talent of mine and bringing me to light. I express my gratefulness to my dear friends who read all my drafts and motivated me to write and express more. I pay my deep sense of appreciation to the editor Saizal Gupta for her wonderful work and for her patience. I would like thank Sornojoy Dutta cover designer for his amazing work. I extend my heart felt obligation to all the members on my publishing team. Thanks to all the people who are partaker for the success for this book.

About the Author

Anything that gets your blood racing is worth doing.

– Hunter.S.Thompson

And Annie calls it passion !!
Annie is charming person who loves to do what her heart always yearns for and she thrives for it. She likes being idealistic and peaceable. Annie did her schooling in C.S.I. Ewart Matriculation Higher Secondary School. It was her second home as she always loves being there. Annie loves her school more than anything because that is where she found hidden talents. It's the place which brought all her hidden talents to light. Currently, Annie is pursuing her B.E. Civil Engineering in Meenakshi Sundararajan Engineering College, the place which thought her life values. Apart from this she is a nature lover and her hobbies are drawing and painting. You can write to her at annjhn.1999@gmail.com or @anniekathy_quotes her Instagram account.

This book comprises all her quotes and poetry which she penned ever since she has chosen writing as her way of letting out her emotions.

Prologue

As I lay down in my bed……
The gentle breeze blew the curtains away
Within seconds I got the view of the dark
sky glittering with twinkling stars
The flickering street light found a way to sneak
peek into my room.

Just when I thought of dozing off to sleep
My mind got electrified with numerous thoughts
They brought back the memories of my darkest nights,
my euphoric days, the betrayals, old friends, the
broken promises, sleepless nights, all my peaks and
troughs .

Yes! My mind was in chaotic
state, Then,

I   scribbled   my
thoughts I poured my
emotions
My tears added meaning to
it, Messed my room with
papers, Papers with LIFE!!!
I took all the bits and pieces of
papers Compiled into a poetry

Indeed! I found peace in
it, I found happiness in it.
I knew my writings will not deceive
me. They will not betray me.
It's just me and my
emotions, Me and my
writings.

YES!! Finally, Art gave peace to my
CHAOTIC MIND.

LOVE

"I am in love for the past 18 years but haven't confessed it" – She said

"Yes! My dear I know", she smiled

 A secret commitment between the mother and daughter.

* * * * *

"Love is fake, Love isn't true, Love Hurts", sighed
a broken heart.
"NO, it is ego that destroys love", corrected
a destructed mind.

"It is not only the umbilical cord that connects
me and her but each and every heartbeat of mine
connects me with her."

-Power of mother's love

* * * * *

As a bird migrate towards food and shelter,
likewise, human soul persuades towards Love
and warmth!!

A Magical Night

As night goes by

Each twilight passes by

With hearts longing

Every heart beat fading

Lost in the thoughts of night

Inner voice lingering in star's light

There comes love to kindle fire

In a magical mysterious attire

Maker of Me

My mom is a diety,
And is a beauty.

My mom is my treasure,
She is my actual pleasure.

Mother's love cannot be justified why,
Other's love is dark and dry.

She take's my pain,
And makes sure it never comes again.

Her care is as high as a tower,
And takes care of me like a
flower.

My MOM Is Maker of Me

I escape from today's reality,
Cause I want to be present in your fantasy.

You know its love,
When you have a soothing feeling just by having
the glimpse or thought of that person.

You gave meaning to my metaphors,
Through you, my personifications
existed, You made my oxymorons true.
But,
Why didn't you give LIFE to the word "LOVE"
in my dictionary?

* * * * *

May be capacitor offers infinite resistance to
DC circuit,
But there is only infinite affinity towards YOU
and ME.

Father's Care

Father's care is high as a mountain
And flows like a fountain

My dad is always smart
And has a wonderful art

His care surrounds me
And his love has a charming look at me

My dad's way is so calm
And always has me in his palm.

The Chaotic Mind

I love
you.
Because,
You became an oasis in my deserted life.

Feeling the breeze over my face,
The sound of wind soothes my
ear,
Closing my ears – imagination flutters beyond
the skies,
Stretching my hands – I feel the world is mine
Yeah !! only dad's bike ride makes me feel fine.

Long distance relationship is like an ocean.
Just like the water is evaporated by the sun,
may be, distance evaporates love but,
just like the rain brings back the water,
loyalty brings back the lost love
Ocean is never deprived of water,
likewise, long distance relationship is never deprived of
love.

*Yeah !! even long-distance relationship makes till
the END!!*

The Chaotic Mind

The twinkle in your eyes,
The charm in your smile
Makes me mesmerized...
Yeah!! I fall for you every
day My love,
My MOM!!

Too many people believe in,
Love of a friend,
Love of a mother, but,
They forget the love of the creator!!

Dear myself,

I know it's hard to ACT as if you are strong, I know you are still a child by heart. But, be brave my heart. Act! Act! Act! till you can. If you can't break yourself for a while. Sob , break down but only to yourself, to your teddy, to your pillow, to your almighty that you believe in, but never to a human! Rebuild yourself, but this time more stronger.

Act again, act more valiant, act stronger. One day your stout- hearted act through all your trials and tribulations will finally mould you stronger.
No more acting then, you are indeed a brave girl now!!

My tombstone will read,
"As I lay her in peace,
In a world full of war and greed,
There lies a soul who fought it with ease".

* * * * *

The instant I saw, children frolicking
My heart asked, "Won't I be happy like them?"
My brain whimpered, "Can you untie the bond of
stress?"
My spirit whispered, "Will I live the life I wish?"
Not knowing what to do
My soul broke out in tears!!

Depth of Agony

Million drops of tears a day

Wounds and bruises tear my heart

Searching for joy on my way

My journey has turned grey

Can someone hear my sobbing?

I' am crushed and shattered in piece

Could you lift me up to the sky?

My soul will find serenity.

As I gaze at the sky
I notice the clouds slowly moving,
As I look deeply into...
All I could think was,
Even I want to move slowly and steadily
Away from negativity and gravitate
towards positivity.

Who am I?
A girl with a brightest smile on her face to hide
her darkest nights.

In the world where people wait for a "Hi" to pop
up, I still wait for a letter from my pen friend.
Old is indeed gold !!

I am not sorry for choosing you as my friend,
I am sorry for myself for believing your words,
Fake friends do help us grow stronger!!

Tear gland broke,
Heart beat faded.
When she realised
that
She was just a "Tool" to his love story.

* * * * *

"Somewhere over the rainbow, I wish I could find my sibling".

- the unheard cry of a single child

He said, " I will be with you forever "
"Should I engrave it on water or
stone?"

      - asked a broken heart

Poets are not always born,
They are the ones...
Who grow with experiences,
Who choose to cry through words.

The Chaotic Mind

I think I got used to getting hurt,
Cause I am able to hold my tears and not let it down!!

* * * * *

Why were you so cheesy?
You said you wouldn't leave
me.
Why was your smile so
deceiving?
You said you wouldn't ditch
me,
"Friends do betray", said a
voice
Oh my! Another broken
heart,
Yes, she sighed with a feeble
voice
Two strangers became good friends!!

The Chaotic Mind

You know my passion is writing,
Yet, you asked me to stop penning,
You asked to stop breathing.

Now,
you want me to live,
How can I ???...
Remember! Words can't be erased,
It hurts! It pains ! It rips our soul!

- From A broken soul.

"Eternalizing my thoughts through words,
Beautifying it through adjectives,
Molding my intensities to metaphors",
Is the way I choose to express my emotions.

*****

I never really understood the meaning of,
"The person who smiles the most has a lot of pain
behind",
until I myself became an eccedentesiast!!

I love to sleep

To escape from reality,

To lull my mind of obnoxious thoughts,

To see happiness (at least in my dreams),

To breathe in peace,

To smile and laugh endlessly,

      ......and my wish list goes on.

The Chaotic Mind

If only love was as strong as hate,
I would have knit you in my heart
But there came your ego as checkmate
Yet I strived to love you, my sweetheart.

If only love was as strong as hate,
You wouldn't have left me
For you, love was time pass delight
Now everyday ends in gloominess.

Cry of A Lonely Soul

Tears and sorrow fill my heart,
Love and joy fill my dreams,
Smiling always – my biggest
lie, As each tear fall as drops.

Though my eyes convey everything,
Faking a smile everywhere,
My soul in sadness hum,
How much can my heart also bear?

Pierced and shattered is my soul,
Burned and weary is my heart,
Summing my life as a whole,
Nothing to say, this is my fate

Heart pumped fast; with tears overwhelming the eyes;
"I pity them", smirked the brain,
Because it knew, he wasn't the one.
...... As he bid his final goodbye.

* * * * *

As generations passed......
Cheesy words were applied on hearts, rather
than spreading it on food stuffs.
.... Are hearts meant to be destroyed and broken??
   Think again!!

WOMEN

"Is being born a girl curse?
Or being poor a fault?
Where is humanity in this universe?
When did humans turned basalt?"

-The unheard cry of a child

* * * * *

"Women are deity's in earth,
Women are goddess from birth"

- said our history

In a society,
Where children are raped,
And I interrogate,
"Why didn't the history repeat itself"??

In 21st century,
We all think of cruelly punishing the criminals.
But, all we could do or speak is
#justice for female infants #justice for women.

* * * * *

Elections neared....
Number of fake promises increased,
Yet, the poor people believed,
The same old politicians!!

Outside my window I see
A lane filled with memories...
From the day,
When I was told, how to walk,
To this day,
When I walk as an independent woman.

*****

Women were worshipped as deities,
Women are treated as dust
Women are thought as a curse,
Though Society play with them....
They grow,
Stronger!
More Daring!
More Audacious!

*- That's the power of **WOMEN!***

Memories

Describe heaven in one word?
Everyone said "SCHOOL".
I interrogated…. "how can heaven be described in
one word??
It's an emotion, feeling that volumes can't withhold.

My wardrobe is a time machine.
Because, those pink pinafores folded in corner of
my wardrobe,
reminded me of the days when smiles and laughter
were real not faked!!

The Chaotic Mind

Just another day
Nope!!
When your heart pumps,
When your eyes see,
When your ears hear,
Remember, you are ALIVE!!
A day is a gift from above,
Not just another day.

If all the weapons in the world could be turned into
musical instruments, then every word will sound like
a beautiful piece of music.
Because, word is the strongest weapon.

You let go off your ego
Start spreading love and happiness
Try to create memories in every little thing you do.
Is the day you realize that you have just one more
year for your college to get over

-Thoughts of a final year

Whenever the memories of my school life flash, all of
a sudden, I feel like am in heaven !!....
But then my mind strikes me with the sad reality that,
Life goes on .... No matter what.

42

As evolution occurred …
History changed!
Our mindset changed!
Technology
developed!
But ART remained immortal and unchanged.

Maturity is When you ask God nothing but
"PEACE OF MIND".
Rather than affluence in this world!

A Days' Song

The clock struck Seven
And the school bell rang
I thought of being in Heaven
But girls pulled me to their gang

The clock struck Three
And the teachers stopped their poem
I thought of being free
With my hearts singing its poem

The clock stuck Five
Mom started her tuition alarm
I thought of being in sky
But I join my friends' arm

The clock stuck Ten
Came home late at night
Had a nice yummy bun
End of the day's fight

Song of Morning

Early in the dawn
I hear the bird's sing

Wakes me at six
In the window sill with sticks

An eye watching sight to view
Is the blue and white Sings the song Ku-Ku
Gives me a strength to grow
And now, blacks in a "V" shape

Shows me the way
And that's the beginning of the day

Unlocking Talents

Few are like sun, always glowing
Few are like stars, always twinkling
But I was a moon, always fading
Need someone to be always aiding.

A child behind the screen
Hasn't seen anything green
Then there came a queen
Her walk was like a sheen.

Found the talents of the child
Unlocked the talents that were filed
And then she gave a smile,
Which made the heart beat so mild.

Her awesome smile meant so much
Her twinkling eyes gave a touch
Brought the Child before the screen
Made her feel, she too a queen.

The Queen of Smile

You are the queen of smile
Your love is like the river of Nile
Your care goes beyond the mile
Your eyes never tell a lie.

You are not just a teacher
You're our hearts teacher
Your teaching has its own feature
You are also our preacher.

You are the God given Angel
Your walk is so graceful
Your words are faithful
Your thoughts are unattainable.

Forgotten Deity

In a world full of fantasies
Where people search for eminence
Found a spirit with humanities
A soul dressed with elegance.

Wondered is she an angel?
Nope!!, she is our mother
A soul much need yet forgotten
A deity that needs to be loved!

MOTHER EARTH

Earth's Whimper

I want to be green and still ,
But I'm sure… that's not your will.
I gave you a vast sky,
You want to make it dry.
You pierce me and give me pain
I want you to stop it, but you do it again
I can't just think about my youth
Why do you harm me? Tell me the truth
I gave you bread
You gave me blood!!

Stop Terrorism! Save earth!

Silent Cry of the Earth

When my blood flowed like a never-ending river...
You didn't realize my worth
In the process of your so called "development"
When my blood turned grey, Then
You realized it was me,
who Quenched your thirst
And, not your developments !!

Don't be blind! Save water, Save your life!!

POWER OF OUR

Abba, Father and Me

I can't do it alone
Lessons so long and test so tough
But I never felt alone
When waves are so hard and rough
I believe that victory is for two
This child and He
I can't walk alone
World so dark with sin
He held my right hand
With faith I'll surely run
I will come out safe with him
My Father and Me.

Your Sins Are Forgiven

Gone are the days of happiness I thought
For I was feeling guilty of my sin
Tears of sorrow filled the pots
Something is pricking me like a thorn.

I heard a still soft voice
Calling, "come my dear"
Not believing gave a pause
Came to know that it was God.

A name that is fame
Saying your sins are forgiven
Tears of joy with thanksgiving
I knew he is always the same.

Undefined !

In search of man ,
Came the Prince of Peace
Knowing that he will...
Get betrayed by his beloved,
Bruised by his brothers,
Forgotten by his Father.
Yet , He chose..
To love the unloved,
To forgive the unforgivable,
To save the unsaved ,
Such is the profoundness of Christ LOVE
Undefined !! Unconditional!!

55

You can contact the Publisher at:

www.fanatixx.in

www.ingramcontent.com/pod-product-compliance
Lightning Source LLC
Chambersburg PA
CBHW051501140726
47987CB00006B/2816